DISNEP PRESENTS A PIXAR

HE INCREDIBLES

maddie

Bring Bake wensnsDay

Adapted by Caleb Burroughs
Illustrated by the Disney Storybook Artists

©Disney Enterprises, Inc./Pixar Animation Studios
Published by
Louis Weber, C.E.O.
Publications International, Ltd.
7373 North Cicero Avenue, Lincolnwood, Illinois 60712
Ground Floor, 59 Gloucester Place, London W1U 8JJ

www.pilbooks.com

Manufactured in China.

8 7 6 5 4 3 2 1

ISBN 1-4127-3939-X

During the golden age of Supers,
there were heroes everywhere. The Supers
stopped bad guys and rescued people who
were in trouble. Two of the greatest
Supers were Mr. Incredible and Elastigirl.

One day, Mr. Incredible was battling
a bank robber named Bomb Voyage
when a young boy interrupted him.
"I'm Incrediboy!" the boy,
Buddy, said. "I'm your biggest fan.
I've invented rocket boots and I
can help you!"
"Go home," said Mr.
Incredible. "I work alone."
Soon, it didn't matter
what he said; the city
didn't want Supers to
help anymore. Their
fights caused too much
damage. Supers had
to live normal lives
like everybody else.

Later, Mr. Incredible and Elastigirl were married. Since they had to lead normal lives, they used the normal names of Bob and Helen Parr.

Years passed and the Parrs had three children: Violet, Dash, and Jack-Jack. The argued like any normal family ... but they were a family with special powers.

One day, a woman named Mirage contacted Bob. She knew he was a Super in hiding and needed his help to battle an out-of-control robot.

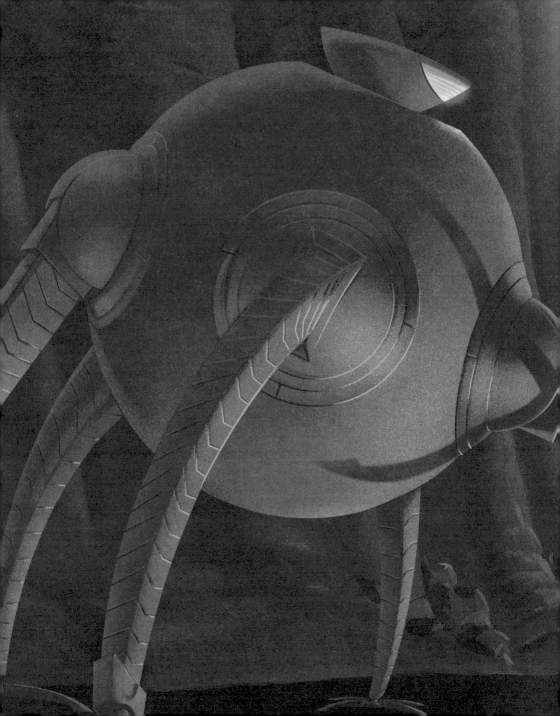

Bob was flown to the secret Island of Nomanisan. There he battled the robot, the Omnidroid 9000. The Omnidroid was a special kind of robot that was able to learn its enemies' weaknesses in order to defeat them.

But Bob was stronger and smarter than the Omnidroid and destroyed it.

Mirage contacted Bob again. Dressed in a new and improved suit, he arrived to battle a new Omnidroid. The robot grabbed Bob and was squeezing him tight when a familiar face appeared. It was Buddy! Except now he was a villain known as Syndrome!

In the meantime, Helen had figured out Bob's secret mission and realized he needed her help. She, too, had a new Super suit.

Helen headed for Nomanisan in a borrowed jet. She didn't know that Violet and Dash were aboard — until it was too late. They were over the ocean when Syndrome's guards shot the jet down.

Helen turned her body into a boat and Dash used his super-speedy legs to motor them ashore.

Once on the island, Helen and the kids rescued Bob. He told them about Syndrome's plan to use the Omnidroid on the city. Syndrome would stop the robot so that he looked like a hero. "We've got to stop him," said Helen.

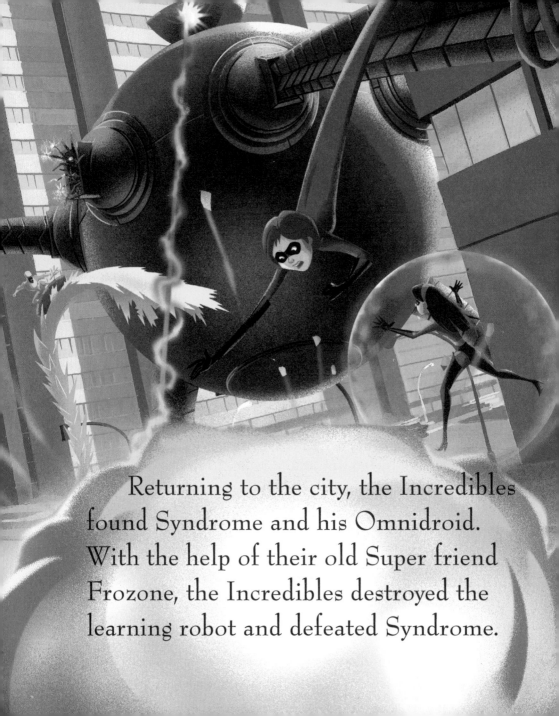

Returning to the city, the Incredibles found Syndrome and his Omnidroid. With the help of their old Super friend Frozone, the Incredibles destroyed the learning robot and defeated Syndrome.

The city was safe once again. All of its citizens were grateful for the help that the Supers had given them. And from that day forth, Supers were allowed to battle evil, rescue those in need, and save the day — every day.